MuSiciaNS

AND THEIR MUSIC

Written by Pauline Scanlon

STECK-VAUGHN

CONTENTS

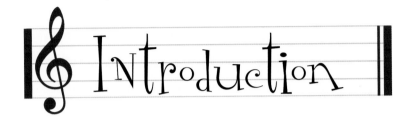

Introduction

Music is all around us. We hear it on the radio, on TV, and on the Internet. It's in movies and computer games. It's played in concert halls, sports arenas, elevators, and stores. Some car horns even play music!

Some **musicians** play musical instruments. Other musicians called **composers** write music. Some musicians play music and write it, too. Of the five musicians in this book, four of them are known for playing at least one instrument. They are all famous composers. One of the musicians also creates new instruments.

Ludwig van Beethoven (LOOD vig vahn BAY toh ven) lived more than two hundred years ago. He came from a family of musicians that had moved from Holland to Germany. *Beethoven* in Dutch means "beet garden." Beethoven played the piano so well that he became a famous **pianist** of his day. Today people remember him for the music he wrote.

Beethoven was able to compose bits of music in his head. He sometimes heard the music of every instrument before he ever recorded a musical note on paper. Then he might go back and change it later. Beethoven's music is still played all over the world.

Scott Joplin played his own music on the piano more than one hundred years ago. Joplin's music came from African rhythms that many people had never heard before. Joplin learned to play the banjo at an early age. Later he studied other instruments. He was best at playing piano.

Music written by Beethoven in his handwriting

Aaron Copland was a famous pianist of his time, too. He wrote new and daring music. Audiences still enjoy his music, much of which was written for dancers.

As all listeners know, music is played on all kinds of instruments. Evelyn Glennie is a musician who plays instruments that most of us have never seen or heard. She even makes many of these instruments herself!

Gloria Estefan uses her voice as her musical instrument. She also writes songs in Spanish and English.

Not everyone can play an instrument or write music. But most of us enjoy listening to the **melodies** all around us. We can also enjoy learning about musicians and their music.

Ludwig Van Beethoven

Ludwig van Beethoven was a famous pianist and composer. His most famous work is his *Fifth Symphony*. A **symphony** is a piece of music that is written for many instruments. Beethoven was one of the greatest composers who ever lived, but in his later years he could not hear the music he wrote.

BEETHOVEN'S LIFE

Beethoven was born in Germany in 1770. By the time he was four years old, he could play the violin, organ, and piano. He played music in public by the age of seven! Beethoven's father, Johann (YO hahn), was a music teacher and musician. Johann gave young Beethoven his first music lessons.

As a child, Beethoven was very shy. However, he loved the piggyback rides his cousins gave him, and he sometimes played tricks on them. Beethoven liked practicing his music more than anything else.

Music thrilled Beethoven, but his life was hard. His mother died when he was very young, and his family was poor. Beethoven had to play music to earn money for himself and his two younger brothers. He also gave piano lessons to younger students. At age 13, Beethoven played music full-time all over Europe. Then something terrible happened.

Beethoven as a young man

When Beethoven was in his late twenties, he realized that he was losing his hearing. He banged harder and harder on the piano, trying to make the sounds loud enough for him to hear. In fact, he banged on the keys so hard that he wore out his piano! He could not hear the notes, no matter how hard he hit the keys.

Beethoven writing music

By the time he was 32, Beethoven was completely deaf. He was able to speak, but people who wanted to talk with him had to write what they wanted to say. They wrote their messages to him on a small chalkboard called a slate.

Although Beethoven could not hear, he composed some of the most powerful and well-known music ever written. How did he do it? Sometimes when we hear a song, the tune stays in our heads. However hard we try, we can't stop thinking about it. We can't stop hearing it. In the same way, composers also hear tunes in their head. They write those tunes on paper.

Beethoven said that he carried his musical thoughts with him for a long time, sometimes years, before he wrote them down. He said that once he created the **theme** of a musical piece, he turned his ideas into sounds that "roared and raged."

A SYMPHONY

A symphony is a musical work that is written for an **orchestra**. Pianos, violins, trumpets, flutes, harps, bassoons, and drums are all orchestra instruments.

An orchestra that plays a symphony may have twenty different kinds of instruments and as many as one hundred performers. The person who leads the orchestra is called the **conductor**.

Symphonies are usually divided into four parts called **movements**. A symphony's movements are like chapters in a book. A reader reads a chapter and then may pause for a moment before going on to the next chapter. In a similar way, a symphony orchestra plays a movement and then pauses before going on

to the next movement. The first movement is fast, the second is slow, and the third has a dance-like quality. The fourth movement is very fast—faster than the first movement. The names of the movements are always written in the Italian language.

BEETHOVEN'S *FIFTH SYMPHONY*

Many people think that Beethoven's *Fifth Symphony* is his **masterpiece.** It was first played for an audience in the winter of 1808. The performance lasted four hours.

A conductor and orchestra

11

The theater had no heat, and the orchestra played badly because the musicians had not had much time to **rehearse**. One listener said that the symphony was too long and too loud. Many people in that freezing theater agreed with him. Today many experts think that Beethoven's *Fifth Symphony* is the best symphony he ever wrote. The *Symphony's* first four notes are probably the most famous opening notes of any symphony ever written.

Beethoven died in 1827 at the age of 56. On the day that he died, a powerful thunderstorm crashed throughout the city. Beethoven's music was thunderous and powerful, too. Beethoven left a huge body of work, including nine symphonies and an **opera,** which is a play that is sung. Musicians continue to play Beethoven's music, and audiences never tire of listening to it.

Scott Joplin

Someone once said that Scott Joplin "just got music out of the air." Scott Joplin is known as the King of Ragtime. He wrote music unlike any that had been written before.

JOPLIN'S EARLY YEARS

Scott Joplin was born around 1867 near Linden, Texas. He was one of six children. His father, Giles, was born a slave but was freed after the Civil War.

Joplin's parents loved music, and both were talented musicians. Giles played the violin. Joplin's mother, Florence, played the banjo. All the Joplin children had musical talent, but Scott was the most talented.

When he was young, Joplin learned to play songs on his mother's banjo. By the age of seven, he could play any **chord** he heard. He could also remember just about every tune he had listened to. While Joplin was still very young, he also learned to play the piano, violin, and cornet. Joplin's mother encouraged his playing.

Joplin's father didn't think that an African-American man could earn a living as a musician, but Joplin's mother did not agree. She worked hard cleaning houses and saved enough money to buy her son an old piano. Joplin practiced on this piano as much as he could.

A postage stamp honoring Joplin

Scott Joplin

Black Heritage USA 20c

When he was 20 years old, Joplin began to travel around the country, playing the piano in boarding houses and dance halls. During this time, a type of music called "ragged time" or simply "ragtime" was popular. Ragtime became Joplin's favorite piano music to play.

Joplin lived on the second floor of this house in Sedalia, Missouri.

Ragtime Music

In ragtime music, part of the tune has a steady beat, while the other part has many different beats. These beats are based on African folk music. Ragtime music was played by African-American musicians in places such as New Orleans, Louisiana, and St. Louis, Missouri. Ragtime was like no other music that most Americans had heard before.

Joplin played popular ragtime music written by other musicians. He also played ragtime music that he wrote himself. He wanted to write his songs down so that other musicians could play them, but he did not know how to write music. He decided to go to school and was accepted into George Smith College in Sedalia, Missouri. No one knows for sure what Joplin studied there, because the college records were lost in a fire.

While he was studying, Joplin played the piano all over Sedalia. He often performed in a club called the Maple Leaf. One of the early ragtime songs that he composed was called "Maple Leaf Rag." It was very popular at the time and is still thought to be his masterpiece.

Joplin made very little money from selling copies of "Maple Leaf Rag" in the first year he published it. Back then, music was not recorded for people to hear. People who wrote music didn't make any money unless they performed the music or published it. When the music was printed and published, it was called sheet music. People bought sheet music so they could play the music themselves. In later years Joplin earned about $360 per year from sales of "Maple Leaf Rag." "Maple Leaf Rag" is still famous for being an unusual and lively tune. It is also quite difficult to play!

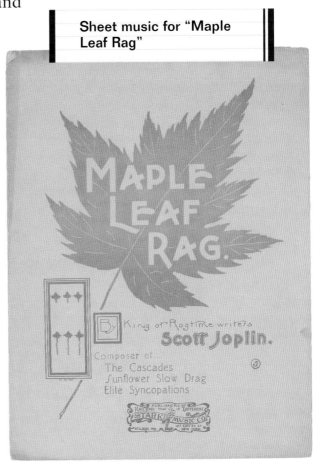

Sheet music for "Maple Leaf Rag"

Joplin's Music

Joplin wrote hundreds of ragtime tunes, but he also wanted to write other kinds of music. He wrote **marches** and **waltzes,** which were not very successful. In 1906 he wrote an opera. It was called *Treemonisha.* This was the first opera ever composed by an African American. It was about a woman named Treemonisha who educated herself and became a leader in her community. She urged the people in her community to get an education so they could have better lives. Treemonisha was like Joplin's mother, who believed education was important.

Joplin's dream was to bring African-American music into concert halls. *Treemonisha* was performed only once during his lifetime. He was very disappointed. In the 1970s *Treemonisha* was finally performed in the big theaters of New York City many years after Joplin died.

In 1907 Joplin wrote an instruction book called *The School of Ragtime.* The book was about the kind of rhythm he used in his songs. Unfortunately for Joplin, ragtime music was no longer popular. Ragtime was also very hard to play, and Joplin's ragtime was harder than most.

Joplin worked hard to convince people that his music was as good as any other music of the time. His music was popular for awhile, but Joplin died in 1917 without being recognized as an important composer. As his wife, Lottie Stokes Joplin, recalled, "He was a great, great man! He wanted to be a real leader. In fact, that's why he was so far ahead of his time. . . . He would often say that he'd never be appreciated until after he was dead."

Almost sixty years after Joplin's death, a 1973 movie called *The Sting* featured Joplin's music. The best-known song from the movie is "The Entertainer."

School of Ragtime

6 EXERCISES FOR PIANO

BY

SCOTT JOPLIN.

Composer of "MAPLE LEAF RAG" etc.

Price 50 cents.

NEW YORK
Published by SCOTT JOPLIN.

Copyright MCMVIII. by Scott Joplin.
English Copyright Secured.

Joplin's book *The School of Ragtime*

Joplin's music won an Academy Award. Three years later he was awarded a Pulitzer Prize for his opera *Treemonisha*. The King of Ragtime finally received the honors that he deserved.

A performance of *Treemonisha*

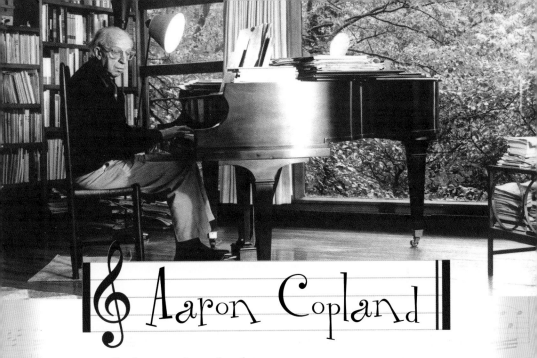

Aaron Copland

Until about a hundred years ago, most composers wrote either popular music or classical music. Classical music is more serious than popular music. It is a kind of art. Popular music is written for a bigger audience. It is meant to entertain lots of people.

Aaron Copland had a great effect on American music and composers. He is best known for the music he wrote for **ballet** dancers.

COPLAND'S LIFE

Aaron Copland was born in 1900 and grew up in Brooklyn, New York. When he was a boy, an older sister, Laurine, gave him piano lessons.

Copland did not like having his sister as his teacher. Laurine was older, so she thought she was smarter and better than he was. Naturally, Aaron did not agree. As a result, the two did more arguing than practicing. Copland begged his mother to get him a professional teacher.

Learning to play the piano was just the beginning for young Aaron Copland. He wanted to be a composer. Copland's choice was an unusual one for an American boy. Few Americans were writing music in those days. Most composers came from Europe.

Copland as a boy

Copland's father was surprised when Aaron said he wanted to learn to compose classical music. But even though he was surprised, Copland's father agreed to pay for Aaron's piano and **composition** lessons. Aaron was even sent to Paris to study, because America had no music schools at that time.

In Paris, Copland studied with a famous teacher named Nadia Boulanger (NAH dee uh BOO lahn jay). He was her first American student. Years later Copland said that being Boulanger's student was the most important event of his life. He always said she was the best teacher he ever had.

BALLET MUSIC

When Copland returned to the United States, he began writing music for dancers. Professional dancers dance to all kinds of music. Sometimes they choose a piece of music they know. At other times dancers ask composers to write a special piece of music for them.

A ballet has two main parts: the dance steps, and the music, which is called the **score**. The director of a **ballet company** asked Copland to write a score for a ballet. This ballet was about a famous outlaw of the Old West.

The director wanted the music to include lines from real cowboy songs.

The ballet music that Copland wrote was called *Billy the Kid.* This ballet became very popular, and so did the music! Soon other dancers asked Copland to write music for their ballets. A woman named Agnes de Mille asked Copland to write a score for her dancers. Her ballet was also about cowboys and life in the Old West. The ballet was called *Rodeo.* Copland's music made the audience feel as though they were in the Old West.

Dancers performing *Rodeo*

Copland's most famous piece of music is the score for a ballet called *Appalachian Spring.* Copland called this piece *Ballet for Martha,* because he wrote it for a dancer named Martha Graham. Graham renamed the music *Appalachian Spring* because she used springtime in the Appalachian Mountains as the setting for the ballet. When people heard the music, many said they could actually see the Appalachian Mountains in springtime. Copland enjoyed hearing this. He had never seen the Appalachian Mountains in spring— or any other time, for that matter!

WHY COPLAND IS FAMOUS

Even though Copland was raised in a big city, he somehow wrote music that made people think of the Old West and pioneers. Copland also liked borrowing from American folk music, jazz, and even Mexican folk music. Some of the music in *Billy the Kid* has small bits of the cowboy songs "Git Along, Little Dogies," "The Old Chisolm Trail," and "Old Paint." Not everyone liked Copland's daring use of all different kinds of music. At one performance, his music was even booed!

Copland in the 1980s

Copland also gave his music a rare sound by using instruments that weren't normally used in classical music. He was not afraid to go where his imagination led him or to borrow from other kinds of music.

Aaron Copland lived to be ninety years old. He once said that the street he grew up on in Brooklyn was plain and drab and had nothing like a pioneer feel to it. Yet much of Copland's music did have a pioneer feel to it. Many people think that Copland was a pioneer himself—a musical pioneer.

Evelyn Glennie

Sitting behind her drums, Evelyn Glennie looks like a rock star, but she's not. She performs in a concert hall and plays classical music. Glennie is the first and only classical **solo percussionist** in the world. A percussionist is someone who strikes, shakes, and rattles things to make music. People who play drums are percussionists. So are people who play cymbals (SIM buhlz), xylophones (ZY luh fohnz), tambourines (tam buhr EENZ), castanets (kas tuh NETZ), bells, and triangles. Glennie has a collection of more than 1400 percussion instruments!

Some percussion instruments

She's always looking for more, too. If she sees something that looks like it might have an interesting sound, she might use it as an instrument. Glennie has been known to use things like flowerpots, animal bones, and parts of automobiles. In addition to all the percussion instruments she plays, she can also play the bagpipes!

PERCUSSION INSTRUMENTS

There are more percussion instruments than any other kind of instruments. The percussion section of a band or orchestra is often called the kitchen because there are percussion instruments of all kinds. Some of them might seem a bit like pots and pans! Percussion instruments are important in music because they sound out the music's rhythm.

Glennie likes strange percussion instruments. She especially likes the boobam, which is made of tubes that are open on one end and closed on the other. If she can't find what she wants, she makes it. She calls one of her many inventions a batonka. A batonka is a funny-looking thing made of pipes. It also makes a funny sound.

Before she performs, Glennie lines up as many as fifty instruments across the front of the stage. It takes an average of four hours to set up all these instruments, and more than two hours to take them down. When she's ready to play, she takes off her shoes and plays the entire concert in bare feet. Glennie plays in this way because she cannot hear. She takes off her shoes so she can feel the music through her lower body.

Glennie sometimes plays all of these instruments during a single performance: cymbals, bells, a pair of bongos, two conga drums, a vibraphone, four wood blocks, and several boobams. As she plays, she leaps from one instrument to another, striking each instrument as she moves.

Young Glennie

Glennie was born in Aberdeen, Scotland, in 1965. She was the youngest of three children and the only girl. She grew up on her parents' farm outside Aberdeen. Glennie's mother played the organ in the local church, but not much music was played at home. The Glennie family did not even own a record player.

Glennie's Hearing Loss

When Glennie was 8 years old, she began to lose her hearing. By the time she was 12, she was almost completely deaf. Although she is not totally deaf, most sounds are muffled to her. For example, when a phone rings, she hears the sound as a faint crackle. Speech is almost impossible for her to hear, although she herself speaks quite clearly. To know what people are saying, Glennie watches their mouth when they speak. This helps her to lip read.

Glennie's teachers knew she wanted to play music and helped her as much as they could. One teacher played the piano in the school music room. Glennie stood outside the room and placed her hands on the wall. When the teacher played, some of the notes made

Glennie's fingers tingle. She could feel other notes all the way up to her wrists! She was eventually able to figure out which notes were high and which were low.

One day Glennie saw a classmate playing drums and asked her teacher for lessons. After a few days, playing the drums felt right for Glennie. She had planned to be a hairdresser until her love of music really took hold.

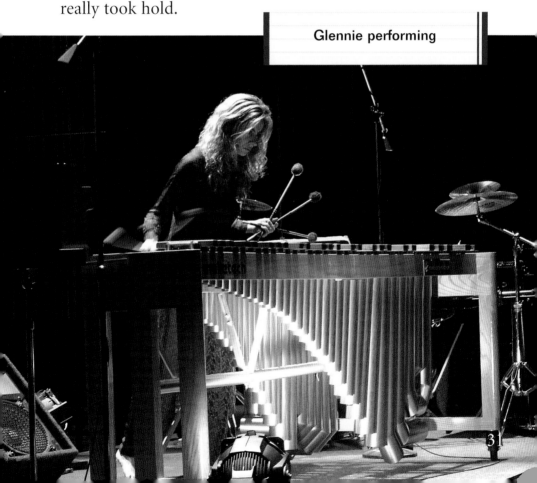

Glennie performing

At age 19 Glennie graduated from the Royal Academy of Music in London, England. There she received the school's highest honor for her work as a composer and musician.

How Glennie "Listens"

When Glennie learns a new piece of music, she does some interesting things. She might hug the speakers while she plays a CD. Or she might place a tape player on her knees. "I don't think in terms of loud and soft," says Glennie. "I think of sounds as thin or fat, strong or weak."

Glennie's Work with Other Musicians

In addition to recording thirteen solo albums and receiving many awards worldwide, Glennie helps students who want to become musicians. She has co-written a series of school music books called *Beat It.*

Glennie feels a strong connection with other musicians who cannot hear. She is president of the Beethoven Fund, which was named for the famous deaf composer, Ludwig van Beethoven. The fund provides musical education for children who cannot hear. Glennie encourages the children to listen *and* play. "I'm not a deaf musician," she says. "I'm a musician who happens to be deaf."

Gloria Estefan

Gloria Estefan has won two Grammy Awards and sold 45 million records. She began singing Cuban music in Spanish and "crossed over" to singing American music in English and became the most successful crossover performer in Latin music history. One of her friends said, "Gloria is a fighter who has never forgotten her Cuban roots."

Her friend was referring to Estefan's fight to become a pop star and to her physical fight, too. In 1990 Estefan was in a car accident and broke her back. Doctors said she probably would never walk again.

Her fans did not agree. They sent her 4000 bunches of flowers, 11,000 telegrams, and 50,000 letters and postcards. Estefan did recover, and she became an even greater star. She is now so famous that she receives mail addressed as "Gloria Estefan, U.S.A."

ESTEFAN'S LIFE

Gloria Estefan was born Gloria Fajardo in Cuba in 1957. Two years later her family moved to Miami. When Estefan was 11 years old, her father became ill and could not work. Her mother got a job teaching at a local school, and Estefan helped take care of her father and her younger sister. While she was taking care of them, she taught herself to play the guitar. She also loved to sing in her room.

Estefan with her husband and children

After Estefan graduated from high school, she went to the University of Miami. Although she was busy studying and helping at home, she found time to sing with a Cuban-American group called the Miami Latin Boys. Little by little, Estefan started singing her own songs. A year and a half later, she officially joined the group, which was renamed Miami Sound Machine.

Estefan took a new name, too. Gloria Fajardo married the group's leader, Emilio Estefan, and became Gloria Estefan. Soon the band changed its name to Gloria Estefan and the Miami Sound Machine. By that time, she had become one of the most popular Latin performers and composers in the world. She is so popular today that she has been voted Hispanic Woman of the Century.

THE GLORIA ESTEFAN FOUNDATION

For Gloria Estefan, singing and composing are only one part of her life. She also spends time helping others. In her own words, "As far as I can remember, my dream in life has been to help as many people as possible. That dream has come true." In 1997 Estefan created the Gloria Estefan Foundation.

Her foundation helps high-school musicians stay in school. It also provides money for those who wish to go to college. The foundation also supports people who are ill. Every year Estefan and her family take part in an AIDS walk that raises millions of dollars to help people with AIDS.

Estefan is proud of her family, her music, and her foundation. She is also proud of her Cuban culture and her American home. A reporter recently asked her whether she felt Cuban or American. Estefan's answer was, "I feel Cuban-American, so I have the best of both worlds. It's a good balance."

Estefan with an award for her music

Glossary

ballet (ba LAY) a kind of dancing that uses special jumps, spins, and movements. A ballet usually tells a story through dance and music.

ballet company (ba LAY KUM puh nee) a group of ballet dancers

chord (KORD) a combination of musical notes

composers (kuhm POHZ uhrz) people who create a piece of music

composition (kahm puh ZI shuhn) the act of writing music

conductor (kuhn DUK tuhr) a person who leads an orchestra

marches (MAR chiz) pieces of music with a strong, steady beat

masterpiece (MAS tuhr pees) a work of art that is considered to be a person's best

melodies (MEL uh deez) musical notes that make up tunes

movements (MOOV muhnts) parts of a symphony

musicians (myoo ZISH uhnz) people who play musical instruments

opera (OP uhr a) a musical play in which the characters sing all or most of their lines

orchestra (ORK uh struh) a group of musicians who play different kinds of instruments together

percussionist (per KUSH uh nist) a person who plays drums or other instruments that are struck or shaken

pianist (PEA uh nist) a person who plays the piano

rehearse (ree HURS) to practice playing a piece of music before a performance

score (skawr) written music that shows each instrument's part

solo (SEW low) performed by one person

symphony (SIM fuh nee) a long musical work written for an orchestra

theme (THEEM) the main melody of a song

waltzes (WAWLTS iz) music for a smooth, gliding dance for couples

INDEX